To Court~
Chelsea, ~~~
"Brittney~

Heroic Animal Tales

sharing a love
of animals and
what they teach us!
Enjoy with Mom Mom
and Pop Pop.

Susan White-Bowden
Jan 16, 1999

Other Books by Susan White-Bowden:
Everything to Live For
From a Healing Heart
Moonbeams Come at Dark Times

These books are non-fiction, personal reflections, written in the wake of the suicide of the author's first husband in 1974, and that of her beloved 17-year-old son in 1977. The books deal with the lessons she learned, the healing process, and the joy that survival, from any deep and tragic loss, can eventually bring.

These books, as well as **Heroic Animal Tales,** can be found in select book stores, or ordered from:
WHITE-BOWDEN ASSOCIATES
2863 Benson Road
Finksburg, Maryland 21048
(410) 833-3280

The Barn Cat, Sassy and a Guardian Angel

Heroic Animal Tales

by

Susan White-Bowden

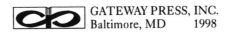
GATEWAY PRESS, INC.
Baltimore, MD   1998

First printing, Spring, 1998

Please direct all correspondence and book orders to:
White-Bowden Associates
2863 Benson Road
Finksburg, Maryland 21048
(410) 833-3280

Library of Congress Cataloging-in-Publication Data:

White-Bowden, Susan, 1939-
    The barn cat, Sassy, and a guardian angel : heroic animal tales / by Susan White-Bowden.
        p.   cm.
    Summary: Three realistic stories about a cat, a pony, and a yellow Labrador dog.
        ISBN 0-9633762-4-1
        1. Cats–Juvenile fiction.   2. Ponies–Juvenile fiction.
    3. Dogs–Juvenile fiction.   4. Children's stories, American.
    [1. Cats–Fiction. 2. Ponies–Fiction. 3. Dogs–Fiction.
    4. Short stories.]   I. Title.
    PZ10.3.W5875Bar   1998
    [Fic]–dc21   98-12830
                                              CIP

Produced for the author by
Gateway Press, Inc.
1001 N. Calvert Street
Baltimore, MD 21202

Typesetting: The LetterEdge
Cover: Janet Kratfel

Printed in the United States of America

DEDICATION

In Memory of Duski

And with love and thanks to my grandchildren, Emily, Brian, David, Jay, Tommy, and Alex. Their comments and suggestions added much to these stories, their enthusiasm sparked the publishing of them.

And as always, with love and thanks to my husband/ editor Jack. "The Barn Cat" was his idea, and as a result of that first "Heroic Animal Tale" the others emerged. "Guardian Angel" turned out to be his favorite, and so we begin the book with that one.

HEROIC ANIMAL TALES

GUARDIAN ANGEL

Told by:
The Listening Spirit
(of Animal Souls)
And by: Angel Herself

The real Angel, and her brother, as puppies.

ONE

❧

When Angel, an eight-week-old yellow Labrador puppy, awoke on this particular day she had a feeling that something very important was going to happen. She didn't know why, or how to describe the feeling. But I gather, from what she told me, it was kind of like the way humans feel, as children, on the very first day of school; nervous, but excited, without knowing what adventure lies ahead. The day, however, didn't start out too well. But let her tell you, in her own words.

(Angel) My mother had pushed my brother and me outside the doghouse, so she could stretch out in the bed. My brother was cuddled up close to me, sleeping late, like he always does. I like to get up early and play. I can't understand how anyone could want to sleep when there's daylight, and so much to do, like chew things.

So there he was just lying there like a dumb dog, so I reached out and grabbed hold of his ear, for a little tug of war. I was really getting into it, shaking my head, and growling fiercely. I had my front feet braced and I was digging in, as hard as I could, with the back ones.

Now, I have to admit I felt a great sense of satisfaction when I realized I could drag the big lug all the way across the dog pen, even though he had started twisting to get away, and was howling in protest—Boy! was he howling. That's when I thought I better let go of his ear. I tried to calm him down, and make him be quiet, but he just kept on yelping.

"Take it easy—for crying out loud. A little tug-of-war won't kill you, and a few 'little' teeth marks aren't going to ruin your handsome, pure-bred, good looks. All right—all right—I'm sorry if I hurt you—Shush up or you'll wake Mom."

(Spirit) But it was too late, as Angel put it, "The deed had been done, and the devil was at the door."

The big black lab mother dog lumbered out of the doghouse, quite annoyed at having been awakened. She growled and sneered at the female pup, sending it scurrying around to the back of the doghouse, to hide. The mother dog nuzzled the whimpering puppy, licked its head and lay down beside it so he could nurse, have his breakfast, and she could go back to sleep.

Angel talked to herself, trying to justify what she had done, while condemning her brother, and criticizing the actions of their mother.

(Angel) "Look at that—that's why he cries all the time—just to get attention—and Mom babies him—just because he looks like her—I know that's it—he can do anything he wants and never gets in trouble. Whereas, I can be the perfect angel, entertaining my brother and building up our muscles with a little tug of war and she gets mad. It's not fair."

(Spirit) As with all young pups, Angel was seeing the situation only from her point of view. She was angry, feeling left out, and unloved. But she was also starting to feel very hungry, and that was making her forget all those other things.

Slowly, sheepishly, she crept out from behind the doghouse, unsure of how she would be received by her mother. The mother dog lifted her head, glanced at Angel without expression, and laid her head back down. Grateful that her mom wasn't one to hold grudges, Angel snuggled in next to her brother to get breakfast. She always felt better with a tummy full of nice warm milk.

Feeling content, full, and once again enjoying the closeness of her family, Angel was just about to fall asleep when she heard voices outside the pen. It was Miss Gabriella, their owner, and some man Angel had never seen before.

(Angel) Mom jumped up and started barking, as she always does with strangers. And my brother and I started barking too. It's fun making a lot of noise, and when Mom does it, she doesn't seem to mind that we're doing it too. With all the noise and everything it was pretty hard to hear what they were saying, but I heard Miss Gabriella say, "The yellow one is the female." And then the man said, "That's perfect, because eventually I want to breed her." Then he said something about his son's birthday, but then I couldn't hear anymore, because they went into the house. When they came back out Miss Gabriella came into the pen, picked me up, took me out, and handed me to the man. He seemed nice. He petted me, and called me my name, but when he put me in his car I got kind of scared. I'd never been in a car before and it made me sick. I threw up all over the back seat.

(Spirit) The man was Joshua Lord, and he had bought Angel to give to his son Jamin for his tenth birthday. The rest of the Lord family included Mrs. Anna Lord, 12-year-old Mary, and a two-year-old boy named John. Mrs. Lord wasn't sure that the family needed, or could handle a puppy right now, with a two-year-old toddler getting into everything. But Mr. Lord had insisted, saying that he had gotten a dog when he was ten, and that it was the best thing that had happened to him as a boy. He said it taught him responsibility, and allowed him to experience the rewards of having an animal as a companion, and that probably the most important thing it taught him was to think about the needs of something, or someone, other than himself. "Until I had a dog," he said, "I was a very selfish kid."

(Angel) I was really glad when that car ride was over. I didn't care if I ever saw the inside of that car again. But I have to tell you, feeling the way I did, sick and kind of dizzy, that I felt even worse when Mr. Lord took me into his house. There was something going on. There were a lot of children running around, mostly boys, and balloons clinging to the ceiling. And there was a cake with fire on top. I took one look at that, and I was out of there. I got as far as the back door, which was closed, and then all I could think of to do was whine like my brother would do. When I turned around I saw that all those kids had followed me, and were staring down at me. Some of them started grabbing at me, and trying to pick me up. And then it happened, I did what I used to do around back of the doghouse. And there I stood in a big puddle, that started running across the kitchen floor. And then Mrs. Lord started screaming. I felt so embarrassed.

TWO

Three months later

The first couple of weeks with the Lord family wasn't exactly a heavenly experience for Angel. She missed her mother; she even missed her dumb brother. But even more than that, after the first day, when everyone was so excited about having a new puppy, it seemed like she had now become more of a bother, than a blessing, especially for Jamin.

Mr. Lord said that it was Jamin's responsibility to take care of Angel; feeding her, cleaning up after her, and housebreaking her. And that it would be Jamin's job to train the dog. Mr. Lord said, "This dog will only be as good as you make her. If you spend a lot of time teaching her, the rewards, of having an obedient dog, will be great. If you don't, you'll have a dog that you can't control, who'll be a nuisance to everyone around her." Mr. Lord had given Jamin a dog-training book, patted him on the shoulder and said, "I'll help if you need me. But a good dog has only one master, and, for this dog, that's you." Jamin had stared down at the eager-looking pup, who seemed to be awaiting her first command. "What? Whadda you want from me? Go chase a stick or something." Jamin picked up a nearby stick and flung it as far as he could. To the boy's surprise the dog bounded after it. However, instead of bringing the stick back, Angel chewed it into little pieces.

(Angel) At first I just wanted to go home. Being with the Lords was kind of like a bad dream. I kept thinking I'd wake up, and I'd be back in the dog pen with my real family. Jamin didn't even like my name. His friends teased him about the "Lords" having a dog named "Angel." But it is my name. Miss Gabriella gave it to me. My whole name is— Guardian Angel of Devilbliss Bluff. It's on my official papers from The American Kennel Club and everything. I'm not just some mutt—you know—I have a pedigree. And when you have a pedigree you get a fancy name to go with it. You see, Miss Gabriella's last name is Devilbliss and Devilbliss Bluff is the name of her farm and kennel. But Jamin didn't like the sound of it. He said Angel was a stupid name; something a girl would call a dog. Just between you and me, I don't think "Jamin" is the greatest boy's name I ever heard; many people don't even know it's pronounced "**Jay**-min." It isn't a name I'd want, but if I could talk I wouldn't say that to him, because I wouldn't want to hurt his feelings.

Anyway, he started calling me "Devil Dog" and I started acting mean, to live up to my name. I thought he'd like me better that way. But he didn't. I was growling at everyone. I even grabbed hold of the meter-reader's pants leg one day, and pretended it was my brother's ear, growling and pulling like crazy. The pants must not have been very good ones, because they ripped almost immediately. Jamin and his mother came running out, screaming at me to stop. I thought they'd be proud of me. Especially since Mrs. Lord is always complaining about the electric bill. But they weren't. They called me a bad dog, and tied me up for the rest of the day.

After that, Jamin's grandfather told him to stop calling me "Devil Dog." He said, "Like people, dogs often become what you call them." He said, "If you name a dog 'Killer' you're really looking for trouble." He said if you're always saying a dog is "bad," it will be bad. But if you look for reasons to praise it and say, "Good dog—good dog," then the dog is more likely to be good.

I liked Jamin's grandfather right away. "Gramps," which is what everyone calls him, has this really nice look in his eyes, like he really cares about you. And you just know by that look, and the soft sound of his deep voice, that he would never be mean to anyone, especially an animal. And when he pets the top of my head it's so gentle and soothing it almost puts me to sleep.

When I first met Gramps I knew everything would be okay. I looked forward to his visits to our house. And then one day Jamin took me to Gramps' house. That was the best day of my entire life. Gramps lives on the other side of the lake, in a log cabin. He used to be a doctor in the big city, and when he retired, he and his wife, Momma Gramps, Jamin calls her, wanted a different way of life. Now he does wood carvings that are sold at a craft store in the little village nearby. He signs the carvings, "The Medicine Man." When he isn't whittling wood he likes to fish in the lake.

And Momma Gramps likes to paint pictures and cook. I think she likes to fix food more than anything else, because whenever Jamin or the other kids come to visit the first thing she says is, "Let me fix you something to eat."

Even if they've just finished lunch she says, "I

know you must be hungry—Children are always hungry—How about a nice piece of chocolate cake, and some cold milk?"

(Spirit) On the day that Angel calls, "The best day of her entire life," Jamin had gotten permission to take Angel on the lake trail, that he often used to go see his grandparents.The trail follows the lake around, through the trees, up over the big boulders, which lead into the pines and Gramps' cabin.

(Angel) When I first saw the lake, I have to tell you, I went a little crazy. My feet started running, and I just forgot all about staying with Jamin, which is what he told me to do. I got going so fast that even if I had wanted to, and I didn't want to, I couldn't have kept myself from running right into that water. It was the best feeling I'd ever had, almost as good as rolling in stinky stuff, after you've been given a bath.

(Spirit) Angel was splashing with her feet and ducking her nose under the water, lifting the cool liquid up, and tossing it around. When she calmed down a little, and regained some of the common dog sense she was born with, she looked up at Jamin standing on the shore. He was laughing. He was enjoying watching her play.

Angel bounded back through the water, jumping

up on Jamin with great excitement, and a big sense of relief. She was so happy that he wasn't angry with her for racing ahead, and jumping into the water without being told it was okay.

"I forgot that Labs are water dogs! I should have brought you down here long before this." Jamin said, as he petted and hugged the wet dog.

"Yeah—yeah!" Angel barked. "This is so-o-o cool."

Jamin picked up a stick and threw it out onto the surface of the lake. Angel lunged back into the water, swimming with great strength and purpose, guided by breeding and instinct, directly to the stick. She gently, carefully clenched it in her teeth. Spinning around in the water, she reversed her direction, and swam, without delay, back to Jamin. This time, she didn't chew the stick, instead she dropped it at his feet, then, shaking off the water, she soaked the boy with the spray. But he didn't care, Jamin laughed, as he half-heartedly tried to jump out of its way. Jamin didn't care about getting wet, it was fun, and anyway he was too impressed with the performance of **his** smart retriever to think about anything else.

He couldn't wait to tell Gramps and all his friends. "Good girl! Good Angel! Here go get it again."

The stick whizzed through the air, landing even

farther out on the lake than before. Angel plunged in after it. The surge of water became a gentle wake as she paddled smoothly, keeping her keen eyes always fixed on the stick, making sure the ripples or current didn't carry it out of her sight.

She was not only happy with the game, but she was delighted that Jamin liked it too. And the best part of all was that Angel felt proud that she had pleased this boy, who she wanted to be her friend.

(Angel) Proud isn't the word—Spirit Lady—I was the happiest hound dog that ever lived. I could hardly keep my four feet on the ground—that is, after I got out of the water. I bounced, jumped and raced all the way to Gramps' house—and you know what? Jamin was running, jumping and racing right with me. Was that a great day—or what? And it wasn't over yet.

(Spirit) Gramps and Momma Gramps were waiting, out on the ridge, when they heard, and then saw, the happy pair bounding up through the pines. They had been worried, because Jamin was taking longer than usual to get from his house to their cabin. But he happily explained the reason for the delay, in great detail, with great excitement, after, of course, Momma Gramps had given everyone, as well as Angel, something to eat.

(Angel) They were all sitting around the kitchen table talking, as people do. Jamin had told Gramps and Momma Gramps more about our water adventure, and what a smart retriever I was, emphasizing that I hadn't had any training. Well, then Gramps started telling Jamin about a Chesapeake Bay Retriever he once had, and what a good dog "Old Rex" was; explaining how he'd swim through icy waters and strong currents to get a downed duck. "Old Rex never let a single bird get away," Gramps told Jamin, "even if it took him an hour to follow it, in the strongest current that ol' river could throw at him—and it could get mighty fierce at times. And then, after he got the duck in his mouth, that dog would turn right around—without even as much as a deep breath—and swim right back through that treacherous tide, to bring that duck back—and then what would he do?"

Jamin just shrugged, because he had learned that when Gramps asked a question, like that, he really didn't want you to answer. He just wanted to make sure you were paying attention. Gramps continued without a pause, "He'd lay that duck right at my feet. Not on the shoreline mind you—not five feet away—No sirree, right at my feet."

The whole time Gramps was talking about "Old Rex," he was shaking his head in disbelief, still amazed that a dog could be that determined to do his job. Well, I figured I'd have to work real hard to live up to the likes of Rex, but right then what I needed was a little nap. So I lay down next to the open kitchen door, where it was nice and cool on the tile floor. I was just about to close my sleepy eyes when I saw him.

A shiny black streak racing across the back yard, and into the wood shed. I was on my feet, out the door, and after him, before I could even wonder how-in-the-world my brother had gotten to Gramps' house.

(Spirit) When Angel took off so quickly, everyone jumped up to see what she was after. Momma Gramps caught a glimpse of it, out of the window, just before it went into the shed. "The cat!" she screamed, "Oh Dear Lord, the dog is going after Blackie."

Jamin high-tailed it for the shed. For you see, ever since Angel had come to live with the Lords, cats had been one of the biggest problems. Angel had been chasing every cat in the neighborhood, every chance she got. She had managed to terrorize the whole feline community. Just last week, Jamin and his friend, had to climb a tree to get a cat, that had gone up there to get away from Angel, and then wouldn't come down on its own. Jamin had tried everything to make Angel leave the cats alone, but she just didn't seem to be able to control herself.

"No! Angel—No! Bad Dog—Come Back Here!" he shouted as he ran.

(Angel) My brother—my brother—I was so excited to see him. I never thought I would ever see him again, and there he was running across Gramps' yard. That's all I could think about. I didn't stop to think if this made any sense—that my brother would be here. I just wanted to see him, and play with him and I'd be real nice to him, because I was so glad to see him again. I wouldn't chew on his ear, and I wouldn't drag him around. I'd give him a big lick, and show him how happy I was that he was here. Into the shed I raced. There he was, sitting there with his back to me. I slid to a stop, almost plowing into him. "Hey dummy—it's me, your beautiful, brilliant sister." Then he turned around. "A CAT!" It wasn't my brother it was a big black CAT! And then you know what that cat did. He raised up his back and rubbed it under my chin. AND THEN— he turned around and rubbed against me again, real friendly like. And I was so shocked I just sat there and let him do it.

(Spirit) When Jamin, with Gramps and Momma Gramps close behind, got around and into the shed, he could hardly believe what he saw. There sat Angel with Blackie the cat cuddled right up next to her. The cat was purring so loudly Jamin could plainly hear him all the way from the doorway. And Angel had this sheepish grin on her face. If Jamin hadn't known better he would have sworn that his dog was blushing with embarrassment. Angel's light golden colored face had taken on a rosy glow.

(Angel) Well, what can I tell you—he didn't run —so there was nothing to chase. The only fun in going after something is seeing how far and how fast it will go to get away from you. This guy's obviously not a scaredy cat, like all those other ones —and he doesn't screech or spit—that really gets on my nerves. It wouldn't take some sharp-eyed, pointy-nose police dog to see that this cat is different, one with admirable qualities and discriminating taste—just look at him—he's crazy about me.

(Spirit) Angel didn't know it but she and Blackie were "soul mates." They had known each other in other lifetimes. We in the spirit world understand these things. Earthly mortals consider such instant, unexplainably close relationships a phenomenon or coincidence.

The cat gently rubbed its head against Angel's shoulder. Then, returning the affection, Angel nuzzled at the cat's neck, finally giving him a big lick right across his whiskered face. Stunned and surprised by what he saw, all Jamin could say was, "WOW—can you beat this?" Even Gramps had to admit that, "No," he didn't have any stories to top this one.

Angel and Blackie played awhile, like two old friends, and when Jamin said it was time to go home, Angel seemed reluctant to leave the cat behind.

"We'll come back soon, girl," Jamin said, "but we have to get home now. Remember, Mom said we're having an early dinner tonight." Jamin explained to Gramps and Momma Gramps that they were going to have a family discussion after dinner tonight. He told them that his mother was going back to her old job at the newspaper, and that they had to work out a few things—like where Angel was going to stay during the day, while he was in school. "And what about little John?" Gramps asked, "who's going to take care of him?"

Gramps and Momma Gramps already knew that their daughter-in-law was planning on going back to work, and it worried them. They were aware that their son didn't help out around the house, as much as he could, or should, and that he often traveled out of town on his job. Anna wanted to go back to work, but it wasn't going to be easy to meet the demands of a job, as well as take care of a house and three children, especially when the youngest was just two years old. "Oh Johnny's all set," Jamin said, "he's going to day-care. It's Angel we don't have a place for."

"Well, she could always come here—especially now that she has such a good friend over here, on this side of the lake."

(Angel) Now there's a great idea! Didn't I tell you Gramps is "The Man"—the coolest dude in the entire family and he's also got one cute CAT. … Do you see why I said, "This was the best day of my entire life."

The real Angel, grown up, at the lake.

THREE

Eight months later

So much happened in just eight months it seems almost impossible to tell you about it in a few words. But using the training we spirits get in condensing generations of information I'll try. After all—I did win a heavenly award for earthly communications; so, with Angel's help here are the highlights.

During the summer Angel and Jamin were never apart. One glorious day after another were spent swimming, ball playing, visiting Gramps, Momma Gramps, and of course Blackie. It made Gramps chuckle to see Jamin, Angel **and** Blackie racing off to the lake to play.

Don't misunderstand, the cat did not go in the water, but he watched his friends from a sunny spot on shore. It was a large flat rock about fifty feet above the surface of the lake. "Blackie's Perch," Jamin called it. From that perch Blackie watched as Angel repeatedly retrieved balls, sticks, and a floating frizbee Gramps had bought for them in town. Blackie would eventually get tired of watching the seemingly endless enthusiasm those two had for water sports, and go to sleep in the sun; having himself a purr-fect little cat nap.

It was the game of hide and seek that Blackie liked. He could climb the tallest tree, and hide between the leaves. Even if Angel found him, and she could almost always follow his scent, she couldn't get up the tree to actually uncover him. As part of the hide-and-seek game, Jamin taught Angel to sit and stay, as if she were counting to fifty; giving Blackie and him time to hide, before Angel took off to sniff them out.

It was a summer of learning and growth for the boy and his dog, and with the fun came mutual respect and love. That summer Jamin learned as much about himself, as he did about Angel. He learned he could teach, that he was capable of being patient and persistent, and how both paid off.

Gramps said, "Jamin did a heap of growing up," that first summer with Angel. But he was still a boy, just as Angel was still a young dog, and things got harder after school started. During the summer, the fact that Mrs. Lord had gone back to work had not caused any problems. Little John was in daycare. Jamin's sister

Mary had been at camp, and when she came home, she spent most days with a girlfriend, and, as you already know, Jamin and Angel spent their time over at Gramps'. When school started, a new routine had to be established. But perhaps I should let Angel tell you that part, because it mostly involved her.

(Angel) Yeah—like what to *do* with me. That's what everybody talked about.

"What are we going to do with Angel? We can't leave her home alone. We can't leave her tied up all day."

I didn't see what the big problem was. They could just let me go visit Gramps and Blackie everyday—problem solved. But no, they thought that was too much trouble—to be dropping me off and picking me up all the time. So what did they do? Mr. Lord had Jamin build a pen for me. He said, "Now Jamin—not only will you be building a safe place for Angel—you'll be learning something about construction in the process. It will be good for you."

Good for Jamin maybe—but what about me? I mean—being in a pen when I was little—with my mother and brother—that was okay—even cozy-like. But, all alone—when you're almost a teen-ager (in dog-years). I mean—HOW B-O-R-I-N-G! What did they expect me to do all day—chew on my nails? One day I got so bored I decided to use those beautiful long nails of mine to dig my way out. I dug this great tunnel under the bottom rail of the pen, and when I was sure that the hole was big enough to escape, I squeezed into it. I got my back under the rail, and the front part of me was free. But that's as far as I got. I guess I'm not as thin as I used to be— too many doggie snacks. I was as stuck as gum on a movie seat.

I couldn't get out, and as hard as I tried I couldn't get myself back in either. I just had to wait for Jamin to get home from school to pull me out. How embarrassing! Then Mr. Lord thought his son needed another lesson in construction, and he had Jamin pour concrete all around the edge of the pen, so I couldn't dig anymore. I went back to just lying around daydreaming about being over at Gramps', and playing hide and seek with Blackie. When I really got bored I practiced my singing. But wouldn't you know it, I got in trouble for that too. Trying to hit those howling high notes caused a neighbor to complain; some man who works at night and sleeps during the day. Seems to me he's the one with the weird behavior, but I was the one who got yelled at.

After school was cool though. Jamin and I played ball. Sometimes when all his friends came by, they'd play keep-away. I'd run from one to the other, try-ing to get the ball; just when I'd get to the one who had the ball he'd throw it to someone else. That wasn't my favorite game, but I played because I didn't want Jamin's friends to think I was a poor sport.

Then we'd go inside and watch TV. That's when I got to show off the new trick Jamin taught me. He taught me to get his favorite soft drink out of the refrigerator, all by myself. Boy did his friends like that. They thought I was the smartest dog they ever saw; especially when I brought them drinks too. It really wasn't that hard to do. Jamin tied a sock on the handle of the refrigerator door. Then he showed me how to pull on the sock with my teeth to open it up. After that, all he did was to put a soft drink can in my mouth and have me carry it into the TV room. Hey—before long he'd just motion toward the kitchen and say, "Get me a drink," and I'd go get it. I mean who couldn't do that—probably even my brother could learn to do that one.

(Spirit) There was one incident in late fall that An-gel has neglected to tell you about. Perhaps she has blocked it out of her mind; perhaps she doesn't even remember it, because of the blow to the head she received. It was a warm November day; a day everyone knew wouldn't return again until next spring. Home from school, Jamin shed his sweater and got out his ball and bat. Angel sat in the shade under a nearby tree, wondering if today she was going to chase the ball or play catch. But Jamin was waiting for his friends to come over. They were going to play a game of baseball. It was that kind of day.

While he waited, Jamin decided to hit a few. He tossed the ball high into the air, and readied the bat from his shoulder. The ball was decending into range. In the fraction of a second it took to swing the bat at the ball, Angel leaped up to grap the ball.

The bat cracked against the side of her head, with the mighty force that Jamin had hoped would send the ball over the outfield fence. With a gut wrenching yelp of pain the dog dropped to the ground. Jamin fell to his knees beside her. "Oh no," he cried out. "Oh no —I'm sorry Angel—I didn't mean to hit you—I didn't see you—please wake up—please be all right."

Angel opened her eyes, but she was dazed, and when she tried to get up she fell back down. With Jamin trying to lift her, Angel stood up again, but she couldn't walk. She couldn't keep her balance. She staggered, falling over again. "Stay down girl—stay here —STAY" he ordered. "I'm going to call Gramps—we've got to get you to the vet."

By the time they got to the veterinarian the left

side of Angel's face was swollen, and her left eye was bloodshot, but she seemed more stable, and fully conscious. Jamin, however, was a wreck. He was terrified that Angel might die, that he had cracked her brain. He knew how hard he had swung the bat, and he knew how sensitive the head was. He had seen a bicycle safety video, that showed why kids should wear helmets. And he knew baseball players always wear helmets when they bat, in case they get hit by a pitched ball.

The vet worked fast to examine Angel, and he tried to reassure Jamin by saying, "She's alert, and that's a good sign. We're going to take her back and do a few X-rays. Try not to worry, I think she's looking pretty good. She just may be a very lucky dog." As hard as he tried, and as much as Gramps patted him on the shoulder, Jamin couldn't stop worrying. It wasn't until Angel ran back into the examining room, and licked the tears from his face, that Jamin felt better. He threw his arms around the neck of his dog and thanked God for answering the prayer he'd said to himself, in the car, on the way to the vet.

"Yes," the vet was saying, "this is a very lucky dog —surviving a blow to the head—like that—without any real trauma—it's a miracle." **Yes**, thought Jamin, **she is a miracle dog—but I'm the lucky one**.

FOUR

❦

The cold winter months brought short days, no ball playing, and Angel got to stay inside. Jamin had gotten permission from his parents to let her spend the day in his room. She tried her best to be good, and most days she was, but sometimes she got so bored she had to chew something. It was usually an old sneaker, that Jamin couldn't wear anymore, so he'd just hide it in the back of his closet without telling anyone. He knew that he shouldn't hide things from his parents, but he didn't want to get Angel in trouble, and, after all, he rationalized, she hadn't chewed anything good that he still needed.

(Angel) I mean—I tried to be good, I really did, and Jamin did everything he could to keep me occupied and out of trouble. He gave me the stuffed animal, that he won at the carnival, to play with and chew on. It was a big ol' ugly blue moose. He started calling it "my friend." I mean—if I had a choice would I pick a friend like that? I once heard Mrs. Lord tell Jamin to make sure his friends were nice, because she said, "People often judge *you* by the friends you keep." Just in case that's true I kept ol' Moosie under the bed most of the time.

Actually, I did get pretty fond of him, and he was fun to chew on. I kept myself busy one day pulling the stuffing out of "my friend." Then I jumped up on the bed and scattered the little pieces of fuzzy white cotton all around the room. It kind of looked like it had snowed in there. I thought that was a fun day. Jamin didn't.

After that Jamin borrowed an old black and white TV from Gramps for me to watch. He'd turn it on before he left for school, and leave it on all day. But, I mean really, how many old Lassie re-runs can you watch before you start thinking you're wasting your life. Watching hero dog wasn't helping my self-esteem. I had to watch OPRAH to make myself feel better. "She" understands that we're not all perfect, and sometimes circumstances can challenge our behavior.

I think the best part of TV is the channel changer. I just love putting my paw on that thing and watch it click away. The faster the better.

Now let me tell you how bad it can be—being a dog cooped up in room with a TV. On what I consider to be the worst day of my life I had watched Lassie, Barney and two Garfield shows. That stupid cat got me so frustrated that I chewed on the bedpost without even realizing I was doing it. And then I tried imitating those dogs in the dog food commercial, chasing that little horse-drawn covered wagon. I got going so fast, jumping over the bed and everything that the room got pretty messed up. And that was just the beginning of the trouble that day. I think the Spirit better tell you the rest. Just thinking about it makes me so nervous my hair starts falling out.

(Spirit) On the day Angel calls, "The worst day of her life," Mr. Lord was out of town on a business trip, Mrs. Lord was at work, Little John was at daycare. Jamin came home on the bus about 3:45, as usual, and Mary got home from Middle School about 4:15. Mrs. Lord had left an after school snack out on the kitchen counter, and a note explaining that she'd be a little late picking up John and getting home, and that Mary should start dinner. Attached were directions for that. The note ended by saying that their father was cutting short his trip, and should be home before she got there. As always, she signed it "Love ya—Mom—Be good and don't forget to feed Angel, and be sure and do your homework **as soon as you get home**."

Jamin came home on time, but he had two friends with him and he never even looked at the note. When he let Angel out of his room she was so glad to be free that she raced through the house. Naturally, the boys chased after her, and to say that they knocked a few things over, and scattered a few rugs would not really describe the disorder they created. The boys finally ended up in front of the television in the living room, while Angel headed for the kitchen. I don't care if all her hair falls out, that dog needs to explain this part.

(Angel) Well you see—it was no one's fault really. Things just kind of happened and got out of hand. Like Mrs. Lord always leaves a doggie snack out for me, along with Mary and Jamin's after-school snack. And since it didn't seem like Jamin was going to give it to me—And I was getting pretty hungry—I decided to get it myself. And when I put my front feet up on the counter to reach for the dog biscuit with my mouth I kind of knocked Mrs. Lord's note into the waste basket—and when I tried to find it I kind of got the trash and garbage all over the floor. And then Jamin called me back to the living room, and motioned for me to get him and his friends a soft drink. Well I got the first two okay, but with the third one, I was rushing, and I must have held it too tightly in my mouth, because I punctured a couple of holes in the can and the soft drink spilled out; all the way from the kitchen to the living room.

I was starting to get this feeling that things were getting a little out of control, and that maybe I should alert Mary. But she had the door to her room closed, because she was talking on the phone, to a friend, like she always does, and didn't want to be disturbed. But I had this feeling she should know what was going on—besides I needed to go out as well. And so I scratched real hard on her door— and the paint sort of came off in strips. It kind of looked like a lion had attacked the door. When she did come out and saw the mess she started yelling at her brother. But still no one was letting me out, so I decided to stand at the front door and bark. I don't know what was the loudest, Mary yelling, the boys laughing, the TV blaring, or me barking. That's when Mr. Lord walked in.

"WHAT IN HEAVEN'S NAME IS GOING ON?" he yelled. Mary got quiet, the boys stopped laughing. Only the TV defied the sudden silence, seeming rude with its continuance. Not only did I stop barking, I ducked out the back door, which Mr. Lord had not closed all the way, in his hurry to get in. I wanted to get out of there, because that tone of voice isn't what you hear when someone is happy to be home, and wants to give you a present he bought while he was away.

"TURN OFF THAT TELEVISION!" I could hear him from outside. "WHERE'S YOUR MOTHER? SHE SHOULD BE HOME BY NOW? Boys you better leave now," he said to Jamin's friends. As they went out, Mrs. Lord, who had just gotten home with Little John, came in. I followed her back in, because it was so cold outside. "Oh Dear Lord— look at this mess!" She turned and glared at me. I slunk down, crawled under the kitchen table, and put my head between my paws.

"Why are you so late?" Mr. Lord said to Mrs. Lord, trying not to yell, but he was.

"I needed to finish an article that had to go to press tonight—but this has nothing to do with me." Mrs. Lord was getting upset now. "I left instructions —these two are certainly old enough, and should be responsible enough to follow them. Where are they? Where's my note? Dinner should be almost ready by now."

Mary and Jamin shrugged. They hadn't seen the note. I covered my eyes with my paws, hoping no one could see me.

(Spirit) *Mr. Lord sent the children to their rooms. "I*

need to talk to your mother in private—and take that dog with you." he yelled at Jamin. **Oh Boy!** Angel thought, **I'm doomed** Jamin hadn't seen his room yet.

Mr. and Mrs. Lord continued to argue, trying to hold down their voices. It didn't work, and Jamin could hear it all, even though he had his pillow over his head. His mom and dad had been doing a lot of arguing lately, and it made him very uncomfortable.

"These children need someone here after school," Mr. Lord continued. "I thought when you went back to work you were going to arrange your schedule so you could do that?"

"I do most days—but sometimes I can't—what about you? They're your children too!"

"My job is more important—after all—we live on **my salary**—yours is just extra—your job is something you **want to do**."

"Like you don't want to do yours? You don't have to travel so much—someone else could make some of the trips."

"My success depends on those trips—it's up to you to make sure things run smoothly at home while I'm away—**that's your job**."

"They usually do," Mrs. Lord lowered her voice even more, but Jamin still heard her. "Mary isn't the problem—she just comes home and talks on the phone—Jamin is the one who needs supervision—and that dog!" Her voice was loud again. "Whose idea was it to get a dog—that's the biggest problem we have—that dog!"

Jamin could feel the tears burn his eyes, and the lump in his throat made it hard to swallow. He shook his head to control the hurt. He wouldn't let himself cry like some baby. **If it weren't for me everything would be all right,** he thought. **If it weren't for me Mom and Dad wouldn't be fighting all the time.**

He needed to get away—he needed to go where he was wanted. He put on his warm coat, a hat and a pair of gloves; lifted the window, and on the way out looked at Angel. "You stay here you dumb dog—I don't need you tagging along—getting me into even more trouble. What good is a dog anyway? Just a lot of trouble—that's all. STAY!"

(Angel) I must have sat there for at least fifteen minutes. Jamin had said "STAY!" and I didn't want to make him any angrier with me than he already was. But he and the Lords were just about to take me to the dogpound anyway. What did I have to lose? I looked at the window, and the cold darkness of a winter evening beyond. Jamin was out there without me. I decided that I was already in so much trouble that a little more wouldn't hurt. I leaped toward the window, ducking my head so I wouldn't cut my pretty little face. The window shattered, I landed on my feet, and was on my way. Oh my it was cold out there—and it was starting to snow. I had to get Jamin's scent before the snow covered his trail. I had it. With my nose on the ground—acting like a little snowplow—I raced across the yard.

Jamin had gone down the familar path toward the lake. That would be dangerous, in the dark, in the snow. I picked up speed. My feet and nose were working faster than ever before. Just as I was about to enter the woods I heard a loud noise. I stopped, and stood frozen in place, to listen and sniff the air.

The noise came again; a kind of rumbling, crackling sound. I flew through the woods. No longer was my nose to the ground. I just raced in the direction of the sound.

At the edge of the ice covered lake I heard him. At first it was weak, a muffled cry, almost a gasping for breath. And then the cry for help echoed across the wide expanse of frozen space. Jamin had gone across the lake, taking a shortcut to Gramps' house and fallen into the frigid waters. He was now encased by ice, unable to pull himself out.

Slowly I crept out across the ice, sliding through the snow that was piling up on the icy surface. My nose up, I had his scent as well. Then I saw him through the darkness. He saw me, "ANGEL— THANK GOD! Come here girl—Let me grab hold of you and you can pull me out." I was almost to him when the ice began to crack under my weight. "Go back—Go back girl."

I moved slowly backward—turned around and went back to shore. A stick—I had seen a large branch by the side of the lake. I grabbed it in my teeth and slid it onto the ice and out toward Jamin. When I got close to him, I used my nose to carefully push the long branch out over the break in the ice so he could easily grab hold of it.

He had it! He was pulling himself out; up onto the edge of the ice. He had one knee out of the water, over the ice. As he shifted his weight to get the other leg out, the large chunk under him gave way, plunging him back into the freezing water.

I tightened my teeth around the end of the branch, holding it secure, so Jamin wouldn't pull it in with him. I was hoping he could hold himself afloat by hanging on to the branch.

Jamin was cold and exhausted, his hands slid off the icy stick, and his head went under. I pulled the branch back onto the ice and began barking as loudly as I could. Jamin came up gasping for breath, clawing for the edge of the broken ice to hold his face out of the water. "It's no use—I can't get out," he said, as if talking to himself. I started barking again. Jamin wasn't a quitter and he needed to be reminded of that. He looked up at me with a half smile, "All right girl—let's try it again."

This time, at the edge of the ice, Jamin stretched his arms out over the ice, and grabbed hold of the branch with both hands. He hoisted his body up as much as he could. His shoulders were out of the water, his chest was resting on the end of the stick. "Pull Angel pull!" he ordered. I sank my teeth hard into the wood and started to back up. Slowly I moved backward, but my feet were slipping on the snow covered ice. I repositioned my hind legs and tried again. In one motion, I yanked on the stick with my mouth and pushed as hard as I could with my front and back feet. My brother popped into my mind. I closed my eyes and pretended that I had hold of my brother's ear.

Pull, I thought, **Pull that big lug across that**

pen—show him how strong you are—pull. I was moving backward. I opened my eyes and Jamin was following me, sliding across the ice on the other end of the stick. "Yes Angel—Good girl—keeping pulling."

FIVE

❧

Angel didn't stop pulling until she felt solid soil under her paws instead of ice. It was a relief to drop the stick, her jaws ached, but she knew that pain was nothing compared to the cold Jamin must be feeling. She ran to him and licked his face. The warmth of her tongue felt hot on his frozen, frost-bitten skin. He hugged his dog, finding comfort from the body heat beneath the snow covered fur, but also in the love he felt toward this animal, who had saved his life.

The relief they both felt would be impossible to describe, especially when they saw the beams of flashlights coming down through the woods, from both directions. Jamin's parents and his grandfather were all on the way.

When Jamin's dad had gone into Jamin's room to get him for dinner, and seen the broken window, he had called Gramps, suspecting that's where Jamin had gone. When Gramps said Jamin wasn't there the search had begun. And if it hadn't been for Angel, what they found might have been very different.

Gramps arrived at the edge of the lake, pulling the old handmade wooden dog sled; the one with the seat and the sides he'd made for Old Rex to pull. Blackie was sitting in the seat. As Gramps was setting out, from the cabin, the cat had jumped aboard; not wanting to be left out, and wanting to help if possible.

Gramps had figured they might need the sled to bring Jamin home, in what shape he didn't know. And that's what scared him. He was sure something must have happened to his grandson. Something must have happened to keep him from reaching the cabin when he should have. He had hoped it would be no more than a sprained ankle, or perhaps a broken leg. He thought maybe Jamin had fallen down the steep slope in the snow. But being a doctor, having seen many tragedies, he came prepared for the worst. All the more reason he felt such joy when he saw his grandson sitting up in the snow. "Thank God—he's alive," Gramps had whispered when he saw him.

When he heard that Jamin had fallen through the ice Gramps insisted that they take Jamin back to his cabin where he had his doctor things. He knew his grandson, at the very least, needed to be treated for hypothermia, which is when the body temperature drops below normal. He wanted to take his blood pressure, and monitor the rate of his heartbeat. Mr. and Mrs. Lord agreed. Mary had stayed home with Little John, they would call her from Gramps' to tell her Jamin was okay.

Everyone was glad that Gramps had thought to bring the sled, because Jamin was too frozen to walk, and a slow trip up to the cabin, in those icy cold wet clothes could have been disastrous. As it was, Angel and Blackie made sure he got there quickly, and warmly. Strapped into the old rope harness Angel pulled with new energy and sense of importance. She bet Old Rex had never been on a life and death mission like this one.

Blackie rode on Jamin's lap and the boy dug his frozen fingers deep into the cat's thick warm fur. Blackie served as a fur muff, or one large mitten, to bring heat and circulation back into Jamin's hands. Gramps says Blackie just may have saved Jamin's fingers.

When Gramps and Mr. Lord were putting Jamin into the sled, and wrapping him in their coats, Jamin had tried to tell them how brave Angel had been and what a remarkable rescue she had performed. But Jamin's teeth were chattering so badly Gramps told him not to talk. He said, "I want to hear every detail of that story—so you just wait until you're thawed out. I'm sure this is a story no one will be able to top." Angel had barked, "Amen," to that, and had then dug her paws into the snow, taking off like the Husky sled dogs she'd seen on TV.

The sled had moved quickly up from the lake, and through the pines, leaving the people to trudge on behind. Angel figured that the story wasn't over yet, and she wanted to make sure it had a happy ending. At the other end of the trip up from the lake, Momma Gramps waited, with dry clothes and hot chocolate for Jamin, and warm milk for Angel and Blackie.

When the rest arrived, everyone gathered in front of a warm fire, with a hot drink and a variety of food served up by Momma Gramps. The food and warmth were a good beginning in getting this family back to normal. Being close to one another was even more important.

Mr. and Mrs. Lord were sitting together at the end of the sofa. Jamin, wrapped in a blanket, was lying down, his head resting on his mother's lap. Mr. Lord was tenderly holding one of his wife's hands. With the other one she stroked their son's shoulder. Angel was curled up on the floor, in front of the fireplace; Blackie snug by her side.

Gramps knew that what had happened, and the

thought of what might have happened, was pulling this family together. He also knew that they needed more than just this one night of being close to keep it this way, and he figured that this was a good time to bring up something he'd been thinking about for several months.

"I have a friend who is a very good family therapist —she is very sharp in helping families sort out their problems and finding solutions that help them function better as a whole. I think she might be very helpful with what you're dealing with right now." Mr. and Mrs. Lord looked at one another and then down at Jamin, who lifted his head to speak to his grandfather. "Do we all go to talk to this therapist?" he asked. "All of us together—as a family?" "That's the way it works best," Gramps said, "Of course you can talk to the counselor individually if you want to."

"We all go," Jamin persisted, "even Angel—she's part of the family." "I would say she is," Mr. Lord agreed. Mrs. Lord nodded her head and smiled. "A lifetime member—she can go anywhere you want her to go."

(Angel) Well when I heard that I sat bolt upright in front of that fireplace, and in two seconds I was off the floor and onto the sofa with the rest of the family. I mean a rug on the floor, especially in front of a nice warm fire is okay, but a comfy sofa is a hundred times better. And as far as going to a therapist, you can count me in. Boy do I have a lot to talk about—starting with: Why did my mother like my brother best—and what about the father I never knew—never even met?

Boy do we have a lot of things to discuss. I wonder if that therapist would recommend that a new **color** TV in Jamin's room would improve my behavior during the day?

You know something? I guess sometimes the worse day of your life can turn into one of the best days of your life.

THE
BARN CAT

ONE

❦

When the Scott family first saw the barn cat Robbie was only eight years old. He had been doing his homework at the kitchen table, when he felt as if someone, or something, was staring at him. Robbie glanced out through the glass in the back door.

"Look, Mom! Come look at the cat on top of dad's truck."

Mrs. Scott had been in the laundry room, folding clothes. She walked to the door to see the cat.

"He looks really hungry, Mom. Can we give him something to eat?"

Mrs. Scott opened the refrigerator to see what they might have to give to the cat. There was some leftover tuna fish.

"He'd like this," she said, as she scraped the tuna into an old plastic cup, that could be thrown away. "You don't want to let a stray animal eat off the same dishes you use," she warned Robbie.

"Why not?" he asked.

"Well, they probably haven't had any shots from a vet to protect them from disease."

"You mean he might be sick?" Robbie asked with alarm.

"Well, he might not be sick, but he might be carrying germs that could make you sick."

When Robbie and his mom went outside with the tuna fish the cat jumped down off the truck, and ran, as fast as he could, toward the barn.

"Hey, where you going? I thought you were hungry?" Robbie called after the cat. "Why's he running away?" Robbie asked his mom.

"He's wild," Mrs. Scott explained. "He doesn't belong to anyone. He's afraid of people; doesn't trust us. He was probably born out in the woods, and never been handled, or petted, by a person. Cats like that live in barns. They hunt mice for food. They rarely get enough to eat, but no matter how hungry they get, they would never risk getting caught just to have a meal. Here, we'll put the cup of tuna on top of your father's truck. We'll go back inside, and, you watch, the cat will come get it, when he's sure we're gone."

Robbie scrunched in the corner by the back door, carefully peeking out of the glass panes in the top part. He was hoping he could see the cat without the cat seeing him. Mrs. Scott huddled close by to watch as well.

Sure enough, the cat slowly crept back to the truck, leaped up on the top, glanced around and began to eat. He was eating so fast Robbie thought, *The cat must not have eaten for days*. Robbie looked up at his mom with a big smile. She smiled back and patted his shoulder.

After that, whenever Mrs. Scott would have something she thought the barn cat might like, such as the oil left over in salmon and tuna cans, she'd put it out for him.

TWO

❧

Two years later

It had been months since Mrs. Scott had last seen the barn cat. But on this day, she got a glimpse of him out of the window over the sink. It was like an orange streak going across the back yard. The cat scooted under the old board fence, that badly needed painting, and ran quickly into the barn, that also needed paint, as well as some major repairs. Mrs. Scott turned to her husband and Robbie, who were sitting at the kitchen table finishing breakfast. Robbie was now ten years old, and in the fifth grade at school.

"That big old barn cat is back," she said with irritation. "We're going to have to trap it, and turn it into the Humane Society. What we don't need, around here now, is another animal looking for food."

Mr. Scott had lost his job when the tractor plant closed down, and he hadn't found another one yet. Many of the farms in the area had been sold, and converted into housing developments, and, with so few farms left, the tractor plant couldn't do enough business to stay open.

Mrs. Scott was working part time at the grocery store, but that didn't bring in nearly enough money to keep the house and the farm running.

They had a flock of sheep, and in a couple of months, when the lambs were big enough to sell, they'd make some money. But right now it was costing money to keep the sheep fed.

Mrs. Scott was feeling a lot of pressure and strain, and had no patience for another hungry animal. Last year, she had let Robbie talk her into adopting an older horse, that a neighbor wanted to get rid of. So now they had old "Dusty" to feed as well. And of course there was the dog, a mixed breed hound dog named "Hank."

Mrs. Scott usually loved having animals around. She was normally a kind and good natured woman. But the worries over money were making her grouchy, and disagreeable.

"Robbie, you haven't been feeding that no-good-stray cat—have you?" she said sternly.

Robbie didn't want to make his mother angry, but he knew he couldn't lie. "Just once in a while —when there are leftovers—I put a little out for him."

Mrs. Scott was very upset. "We don't have any leftovers anymore. We need everything we have. I'm not buying food for some stray cat, that does nothing to earn his keep around here."

Mrs. Scott could see that Robbie felt awful about doing something that upset her so much, and that made her feel guilty about yelling at him. She started to cry.

"I'm sorry, Mom."

She turned away, and picked up a dish towel to wipe away the tears. "It's not your fault," she said.

Mr. Scott got up from the table, and put his arms around his wife. "It'll be all right, soon. I'm sure to get a new job before long. I'm going into the city this afternoon to talk to the lawn tractor people. Maybe they'll have a job I can do."

THREE

The real Barn Cat in the hayloft.

That afternoon, when Mrs. Scott went out to the barn to feed the sheep she was still thinking about the bills that needed to be paid, and how she might be able to get a full-time job. She was not concentrating on what she was doing, and not being as careful as she should.

She had been up in the top part of the barn, to throw down several bales of hay; two for the sheep, and one for the horse. Then, carrying a bag of feed, Mrs. Scott started back down the steep steps. Half way down, one foot slipped on some loose hay. Because of the heavy bag of feed in her arms she lost her balance. As she fell, her leg slid between two of the steps. In an effort to avoid having the bag of feed fall on top of her, she let go and flung herself away from it. In doing so, the pinned leg twisted with a powerful jerk. She heard it snap.

When Mrs. Scott's head and shoulders hit the floor of the barn, at the bottom of the steps, she could feel the terrible pain. Her leg was caught, and she knew it was broken. She was hanging upside down and she couldn't move.

"Help," she screamed out in agony. "Help me —someone help me."

Why am I yelling, she thought. *No one is home, and even if they were they couldn't hear me.*

Dusty the horse looked at her over the stall door, but there was nothing he could do. The sheep baaed in the barnyard. Certainly they couldn't help. Hank, the hound dog, was nowhere around. He was probably out chasing rabbits in the woods. Mrs. Scott moaned in pain, and rolled her head around, not knowing what to do.

From where she lay, Mrs. Scott could see up the

stairs to the top of the hayloft, and there sat the barn cat, looking down at her.

"Well don't just sit there—do something," she shouted, irritatedly, because she knew that there was nothing the cat could do either. Her voice must have startled the cat, because he jumped down, and ran out of the barn.

"What am I going to do," Mrs. Scott said aloud, beginning to panic. The pain was terrible, and her leg was starting to swell.

Eventually Robbie got home from school. His father's pickup truck was gone, and when he called out for his mother, she didn't answer. He figured that maybe she had gone with his dad. She usually left a note when she did that, but, he thought, she probably forgot. With all the worries she'd had lately it would be understandable.

Robbie opened the refrigerator door to look for a snack. He was really hungry. Just as he started fixing a peanut butter sandwich, he heard a loud yowling coming from the tree next to the kitchen window.

The barn cat was sitting on a limb of the tree right outside the window. That was the closest the cat had ever been to the house. He was yowling and yowling, as loud as he could.

Oh boy, thought Robbie, *I guess you're really hungry too. But, Mom will get very mad if I feed you, after what she said this morning.*

The cat continued to meow as loud as he could. Robbie was feeling very sorry for him, and started looking around for something he could give the cat that his mother wouldn't miss. He wondered if cats liked peanut butter. He broke off a piece of his sandwich, and took it outside.

As soon as Robbie came out the cat jumped down and headed for the barn, just as it always did. But when Robbie went back inside to watch, while the cat determined it was safe to come get the food, the cat stayed on the other side of the fence, and again started to meow loudly. He had never done that before.

Robbie went outside again, picked up the piece of sandwich, and walked toward the cat holding it out. "Here you silly cat. Here's something to eat."

When Robbie got through the gate, and close to the cat, it again darted away, this time into the lower part of the barn.

"Why are you going down there? I thought you liked the hayloft?"

After Robbie made his way through all the noisy sheep in the barnyard, he heard his mom.

"Robbie, help me." Her voice was weak now, and filled with pain. When Robbie saw his mother he was frightened, and afraid that she might be dying. But she quickly reassured him by telling him that it was just her leg that was hurt. Mrs. Scott then told Robbie not to try and get her up, but to go back in the house and call 911.

The medics arrived in a few minutes, and worked quickly to free her. They then put her on a stretcher, and strapped the injured leg. The barn cat watched it all, from the hayloft. Robbie noticed him and so did Mrs. Scott. It was then that Robbie told his mother how the cat had meowed, and led him out to the barn.

Robbie went to the hospital with his mother, and he held her hand as her leg was set in a cast. Then the ambulance driver brought them back home, and helped her inside.

When Mr. Scott arrived home that night, he burst through the door shouting enthusiastically that he had gotten the job. Then he stopped abruptly—shocked as he saw his wife with her leg in a cast, propped up on the sofa.

"What happened?" he said with alarm, rushing to her side.

She told him the whole story, then asked him to tell her about his new job. Her excitment matched his.

Then Robbie walked into the living room from the kitchen. "Come see what I made," he said.

Mr. Scott helped his wife get up, putting his arm around her so she could hobble across the room. In the kitchen, Robbie opened the refrigerator door, and took out a little cake. Mr. Scott looked puzzled. "How did you know there would be good news to celebrate tonight? How did you know I would get the job?"

"This isn't for us," Robbie said. "It's made out of tuna fish, and the icing is cream cheese. Mom said I should make it." Robbie held out the cake for his father to see. On the top of the cake Robbie had used pieces of tuna fish to spell out—THE BARN CAT.

Outside, the barn cat had hopped up on top of Mr. Scott's pickup truck, and was watching through the glass in the back door. The barn cat seemed to be smiling.

REMEMBERING
SASSY

The real Sassy in the barnyard.

ONE

❧

As with all things that turn out to have a profound affect on your life, Sassy was a pony I'll never forget, and should never forget. That's why I'm telling you this story.

My name is Elizabeth Wordley, but my grandchildren call me Mums, and now everyone I know calls me that. And you know something? I like that the best of any name I've ever had. It was my granddaughter, Brooke, who started calling me Mums. She was my first grandchild, and, as you probably know, what the first one does they all do. "Mums the Wordley," is what they now say, as a joke, because I'm not often quiet. I'm never mum about anything. I usually have something to say about everything; sometimes quite a lot. Like now, and once again I've gotten off track. This is a tale about Sassy, not me. And it began when Brooke was 7 years old, and had just started taking riding lessons.

We had gone to a horse auction, that Brooke's riding teacher, Miss Joan, had told us about. A riding school was going out of business, and selling all of its horses and ponies. We were hoping to find a pony that would be suitable for Brooke. She had only been riding for a couple of months, and hadn't done much trotting and cantering, so she needed a well trained pony, that was both older, and more experienced than she.

Another concern was finding a pony I could afford. I'm a widow. My husband died several years ago, and I have to be very careful about budgeting the money he left me, along with my Social Security benefits. I had been saving for a pony ever since Brooke started to ride, but I figured $500 was the most I *should* spend. $1,000 was the absolute most I *could* spend.

When Brooke and I arrived we could feel the excitement, and quickly got caught up in the rush of activity. The auction pavilion had a large center ring, with raised bleachers on two sides. The back of the ring led to the stalls where the horses and ponies were kept. Beyond that, outside, was a riding ring where people were trying out some of the horses they were interested in buying.

Miss Joan was leaning on the fence, by the outside ring, watching an adult student of hers riding a big bay Quarter Horse. She waved when she saw us, and we rushed over to her. Brooke was beside herself with anticipation. "Where are the ponies, Miss Joan? Have you seen one for me? What color is it? Is it a boy or girl?"

Miss Joan laughed at Brooke's impatience, but was pleased with her enthusiasm over the prospect of having her own pony.

"Hold on," she said, patting Brooke on the shoulder, "I have seen several—but first what are the proper names for a girl horse and a boy horse?"

Brooke tried to calm herself down long enough to answer. "A girl would be a filly, if she's young, or a mare if she's over two years old. A boy would be a colt, or a stallion, or a gelding if he's been altered so he can't father a baby."

"Very good! Now what is a baby horse called —no matter if it's male or female?"

"A foal!" Brooke shouted happily, jumping up and down. "Now can I go see the ponies?"

"They're in the stalls at the end of that shed," Miss Joan said, pointing to the long building attached to the arena, "but be careful—remember you don't know them and they don't know you —they might kick or bite."

There was a sleek, shiny black pony named Raven's Wing and a little white pony, that Miss Joan said was actually gray, named Country Mouse. Miss Joan told Brooke that Country Mouse was too small, that she'd outgrow him very quickly. She said Brooke needed a pony that measured at least twelve hands.

The height of horses and ponies is measured from the ground to the highest point on the backbone, which is called the withers. It's in front of where you sit on the horse's back, right where the mane ends. The measurement used is called hands. One hand equals four inches. A pony can be anything up to fourteen hands, two inches. Anything over that is considered a horse. Country Mouse was only about ten hands.

The pony Brooke thought was the prettiest was a bright red chestnut, with a white star on her forehead, named Star Gazer. Her coat was just about the same color as Brooke's hair. Maybe that's why Brooke was attracted to her. Star Gazer was twelve hands, two inches, just the right size. And the pony was fifteen years old, with enough experience to be gentle, and manageable, for a beginner, such as Brooke.

I was the first one to notice Sassy. She was turned away from us, facing the back of the stall, her head down, and quietly munching hay. She was the right size, about thirteen hands. She had a dark brown coat, that was a little shaggy; not smooth and shiny like Star Gazer, or Raven's Wing.

"Look over here," I called out to Brooke, who was still hanging over the gate petting Star Gazer. She jumped down and climbed up to look into Sassy's stall. "He's all fuzzy, like a stuffed animal."

I laughed, because that's exactly what this pony looked like, a big stuffed animal. "It's not a he," I said, "it's a she. And the sales program says that her name is Sassafras."

"Sassafras?" Brooke said, scrunching up her face like a question mark. "What kind of name is that?"

"Sassafras is a type of tree, and Sassafras root is often used to make tea or herbal medicine. It can be very soothing. Some think Sassafras has healing powers."

"Why would anyone name a pony that?"

"I don't know—maybe because her coat is the same color as the bark on the Sassafras tree. Or," I said, my voice wavering dramatically, "maybe she possesses a magic spirit."

At that point Sassy must have been tired of us talking about her behind her back, because she moved around to face us, lifting her head to nuzzle at Brooke's outstretched hand. "OHH—look Mums—she likes me."

Sassy had a big, wide, white blaze that ran down the front of her face, ending at her pink nose. There was also white on both hind legs, like two long knee socks. But what you noticed most about this pony were her big dark eyes, that seemed to convey a kindness, and deep intelligence.

Miss Joan now joined us at Sassy's stall. "You like this one?"

"She's cute," Brooke said, "and she likes me— look." Brooke put her hand out again and Sassy gently nibbled at it.

"I asked the riding school owners about her," Miss Joan said. "She's part Thoroughbred and part Welsh pony—that's why she has the long coat. She's had a wonderful career—done a lot of showing—won a lot of ribbons—has lots of experience—too much actually, that's the problem— she's a very old pony—twenty-eight. You need a younger one—that will last at least five years, and have enough energy to be ridden every day. There's no telling how long a pony this age will last—could go lame any time—or have a heart attack. One of the others you've looked at would be a better investment—of your time, as well as your money. This pony could die tomorrow."

Brooke's expression turned sad, as she pulled her hand back and climbed down. Sassy hung her head, turning back around to resume eating hay.

In the sales pavilion the auction had begun. The stands were almost filled on both sides. Climbing past the people already in place, Brooke and I found a space just big enough for the two of us, near the top of the bleachers, on the right side of the ring. Miss Joan stayed down by the ring, to be closer to the horses and ponies, and to help with sales details, if any of her students were lucky enough to get the horse or pony they were bidding on.

At the corner of the ring the auctioneer spoke into a hand held microphone. As the horses were ridden around, in front of the stands, he described each of them, and their backgrounds. Then he took bids from the people who wanted to buy them.

Some of the horses were sold first, then the ponies, followed by the rest of the horses. The horses were selling for thousands of dollars each. As we waited, Brooke was growing restless, and I was getting disheartened, realizing that the chance of any of them selling for a price I could afford was very slim. As the selling of the ponies began, Brooke was making her way back up the bleachers, with a hotdog in one hand, and a soft drink in the other.

"Hurry up, Brooke," I called out, "look there's Star Gazer." A teen-aged boy was riding her. He trotted the pony into the ring, then by tightening his legs, and kicking her slightly, he smoothly guided her into an easy canter. A murmur of admiration went up from the crowd.

"A true champion," the auctioneer was saying, "if you want a good show pony this is it. Star Gazer has won many blue ribbons," he said, "and at just fifteen years of age she will win even more in the years to come. What is the opening bid on this splendid animal." A hand went up across the arena, and a man yelled out, "Fifteen hundred—a hundred for each of her years."

The auctioneer laughed into the microphone, as if what the man had said was a joke, "That's very nice, but you and I, and everyone here, knows that this pony is worth a thousand for each of her years."

My heart sank. The highest bid for Star Gazer was not fifteen thousand, but it was five thousand. Next came Raven's Wing. He sold for three thousand five hundred. I looked over at Brooke, "I'm afraid we're not going to get a pony today," I said. She shrugged, as if she understood, but I saw tears forming in her eyes, before she looked away.

When Sassy came out Brooke and I both gasped with surprise because she looked so spirited and youthful. The same teen-aged boy, who had ridden Star Gazer, was riding her. Sassy trotted around the ring, with long smooth strides, her head held high, her ears up, her eyes looking straight ahead.

As the boy had done with Star Gazer, he nudged Sassy into a canter, and then he did something that he hadn't done before, he urged Sassy into a full gallop.

She flew around the arena like a young race horse, charging out of the ring, spinning, and then racing back into the center of the pavilion, where the rider pulled her to a complete and sudden stop. She stood like a statue, until the boy pulled gently back on the reins, which caused Sassy to move backward four steps, and stop again. The crowd cheered, and Sassy acknowledged their approval by tossing her head. She was a true show horse, with the two things necessary to be a champion—years of experience, and, probably more importantly, she loved performing. Sassafras loved being in the spotlight. But at her age, were her show days over?

The auctioneer's voice came booming over the loud speaker, "Well! What we have here is a mighty fine pony—there can be no doubt in anyone's mind after that demonstration. But we are not going to mislead any one either—The owners have been very honest about this pony—oh they could have tried to pass her off as a younger pony, because she sure looks and acts like a young filly, doesn't she?" The crowd applauded. "That's because there is still a lot of life, and perhaps many good years, still left in this old girl, but she is twenty eight years old. However, for the right person Sassafras is going to be a mighty fine buy. Now who's going to start the bidding?" No one said anything. I looked at Brooke, and she had that pleading look on her face, which she gets when she wants something really badly. Now, I'd never bought anything at an auction before, and, even though I've already told you I'm not shy about speaking out, somehow I felt intimidated.

But Brooke had grabbed my hand, and then she whispered, "Please, Mums." And all of a sudden I felt my other hand go up, and heard myself yelling, "Two hundred dollars"—the lowest bid of the day. The auctioneer didn't laugh, but you could tell that he expected someone to offer more than that for such a fine pony.

"Well now we have an opening bid—two hundred dollars from the lady and the little girl at the top of the stands over there," he said, pointing our way. "Is that your daughter?" he asked, being polite, and not assuming I was old enough to be a grandmother. "My granddaughter," I said, not to loudly. "What was that?" he asked. "It's her granddaughter," the people in the stands around us called out. I laughed, and Brooke hugged my arm, a little embarrassed that everyone was looking at us. "All right," the auctioneer continued, "we have an opening bid, but surely the rest of you are not going to pass up the opportunity to buy a fine pony like …"

"Three hundred," a man yelled out from the bottom row.

"Three-fifty," another said from the other side.

The auctioneer looked up at me. "Four-fifty!" I called out a little louder this time.

He looked at the man below us, "Five hundred," the man said.

"Six-hundred" said the man on the other side. "Now we're cooking," said the auctioneer, "do I hear six-fifty?"

He looked at the man below us. The man shook his head no; he was out of the bidding. The auctioneer looked up at me. I looked at Brooke, and then I looked down at Miss Joan, who shrugged, seeming to say "if you want her, go for it"

"Seven hundred!" I yelled out. That was as high as I was going to go. "Do I hear seven-fifty?" The auctioneer yelled into the microphone. The man on the other side hesitated, then shook his head no. "Is that it then?" continued the auctioneer, "Are you all done? Seven hundred dollars for Sassafras?

—Ten years ago you would have been paying seven thousand for this pony, and calling it a steal—now it's seven hundred! All right—going once—seven hundred; going twice—ladies and gentlemen— boys and girls—this is a wonderful pony—and this is your last chance—seven hundred the third and last time—Gone—sold to the lady and her granddaughter in the top of the stands." I looked over at Brooke, "Well you have yourself a pony." She threw her arms around my neck, and the whole arena erupted in a cheer.

TWO

❦

From the very first day we had her, Sassy was everything that anyone could ever hope for in a child's pony. I repeatedly told everyone who would listen, "The money I paid for that pony was the best seven hundred dollars I *ever* spent."

Sassy was as kind and gentle, and as smart, as those soft brown eyes indicated she would be. And the wisdom, she had gained from all her experience, she used to help teach Brooke to become confident and at ease about riding.

The day after we brought Sassy home, to my farm, Brooke came over with her family to try her out. Brooke's father is my son. He and his wife, along with Brooke, and their other two children, another girl who's 3 and a 4-year-old boy, live about ten minutes away in a new housing development. They have a nice house, with a large backyard, but it's not big enough to keep a pony. Besides "Charlie Horse," the Quarter Horse that was my husband's, needed some company, and I was sure that Sassy would be a good companion for him, as well as for Brooke. Also, I was going to start riding again, something I hadn't done for a long time, and then Brooke on Sassy, Charlie Horse and I, could go out on the trails together.

Well, on this first day, when Brooke and I went out to the barn to get Sassy ready to ride we immediately began to realize what a true gem we had. Sometimes it's really hard for children to bridle a pony. You have to get the bit in the pony's mouth, and then quickly get the top of the bridle over its ears. If the pony moves its head around, or pulls away from the child it's almost impossible for them accomplish this task alone. I once watched a little girl, standing on her tip toes, trying to pull a horse's head down, so she could slip the top of the bridle over its ears. She almost had it over, when the horse suddenly threw its head back, lifting the child right up off the ground. The poor kid was hanging on, dangling from the horse's head, her feet about 12 inches off the ground.

Despite this image in my mind, I decided to see if Brooke could bridle Sassy all by herself. As it turned out she didn't have to do anything except stand in front of Sassy with the bridle in her hands. The pony bent her head down, took the bit in her mouth, while Brooke easily slipped the top, "headpiece," over her ears.

"Look at that, Mums," Brooke said happily, "Sassy is so smart she can almost put her own bridle on." And that was just Sassy's first demonstration of *how* smart she was.

Brooke started out by riding Sassy around the paddock, just walking and getting the feel of the pony's stride and body movements. Brooke had the biggest smile on her face, and she kept patting Sassy on the neck, saying, "Good girl—good Sassy, I can't believe you're really *my* pony. Oh Mums I love this pony so-o-o much." Which, of course, put a big smile on my face. When she felt ready to move on, Brooke walked Sassy up to the field, where it's flat, with more space, to try trotting. We all followed along, like a little parade. The little kids were jumping and laughing, and asking when they could get a ride. Their dad kept saying, "Now be careful Brooke, you don't know this pony yet, and she doesn't know you—Be ready just in case she shies at something."

None of this bothered Sassy. She stayed calm, and just walked along, looking around at her new home. It was such a beautiful, warm and sunny day, the first day of spring, March 21st. The birds, in the hedgerow, were singing. And even though the field still carried the drab shades of winter, fresh green shoots of grass were starting to grow out of the old brown clumps, left over from last year.

After walking once around the top of the field Brooke gave Sassy a little kick with both feet. "Trot, Sassy, TROT!" she said with authority, as Miss Joan had taught her to do. Sassy eased into a nice slow trot. Her legs stretching out smoothly, her hoofs just gliding over the top of the grass.

Brooke's father was getting nervous. He never did take to riding, even though I had gotten him to take a few lessons when he was a boy. He always said he felt more in control on his bicycle, and it got him where he wanted to go just as fast as a horse. *And* he didn't have to feed the bicycle, *or* clean out the shed where he kept it.

"Mums," my son said, anxiously, "do you really think Brooke should be going that fast, on a pony she's never ridden before?" My son had a point.

Sassy, was obviously feeling good on that lovely spring day, and also probably trying to show off a little bit, for her new owners. Afterall, we did see, at the auction, that Sassy loved to perform. But Brooke was doing a pretty good job of keeping up with the increased speed and rhythm of the trot. But then the up and down motion, called posting, became a little erratic. Just as I was about to call out for Brooke to bring Sassy back to a walk, Brooke lost her balance. One foot came out of the stirrup, and her weight shifted. Sassy felt it too. As Brooke grabbed on to the pommel (the front of the saddle) to steady herself, and keep from falling off, Sassy gradually slowed to a walk, and then came to a stop. And there the pony stood quietly, until Brooke got her foot back in the stirrup, regained her composure, and told Sassy to, "Walk on!"

My son looked over at me, shook his head, and said, "If I'd had a pony like that, I might have been willing to clean out a stall to learn to ride." Never again did he worry about Brooke being safe on Sassy.

Over the happy months that followed there were many more memorable incidents, as Brooke learned more about riding, and she and Sassy became close friends. Brooke enjoyed just going to the barn, brushing Sassy, and braiding her mane. She didn't even seem to mind cleaning out the stall. In fact, I think she liked spreading fresh straw, and giving Sassy lots of sweet smelling hay to make her comfortable and content. I'd often find Brooke sitting in the clean stall with Sassy, chewing on a piece of hay herself, talking to the pony as if it were her best friend. As for me, I got to see a great deal of my granddaughter, and that alone was worth the seven hundred dollars Sassy cost.

Every Wednesday afternoon Brooke had her riding lesson with Miss Joan. Brooke wanted to take the lesson on Sassy. I didn't want to spend the money to board the pony at the riding school, so I borrowed a little trailer from our friend, and neighbor, Mr. Gil. It was a narrow one horse trailer that Mr. Gil had built himself. This cute little trailer was painted white, and had a green canvas top, that was arched, making it look very much like a little covered wagon.

In fact he had used it in a bicentennial cele-bration in 1976. On the side of the trailer was a sign saying, "Bicentennial Wagon Train to Penn-sylvania."

I hitched it to the old four-wheel drive farm truck, and every time we drove into Miss Joan's, we generated smiles and even a few chuckles. I was sure that Sassy had been accustomed to a more stylish mode of transportation, expensive padded trailers. But she didn't seem to mind this less glamorous way of traveling. In fact she seemed to be enjoying herself. Each time, she walked into the trailer all by herself, and once inside she stood perfectly still. We didn't even have to tie her up. And when we got to the riding school, and opened the tailgate, she backed out, all by herself. It was like her own personal stall on wheels, that she didn't have to share with anybody else.

After several months of lessons with Sassy, Miss Joan thought it would be a good idea for Brooke to enter a pony show.

"I think it would do Brooke good to get the experience—She shouldn't expect to win a ribbon," Miss Joan said, "since this will be her first time, and she's still got a lot to learn, and she's sure to be nervous. But it would be a good experience."

So off we went, early one Saturday morning, Brooke and I in the farm truck, with the saddle and bridle and all the rest of the gear stacked carefully in the back. Sassy, in her covered wagon, trailed along behind.

It was a beautifully warm day, and our spirits were high, and we began singing "Zippidy-Do-Da," and other old favorites, as loud as we could. The truck's windows were open, so Sassy couldn't help but hear us. When I looked in the rear view mirror I swear it appeared as if the pony were swinging her head to the rhythm of the songs, and even, perhaps, humming along.

Brooke had spent the night at my house, and had gotten up very early, to groom Sassy until her furry coat almost shone, and together we had braided her mane and tail and tied on little pink ribbons. We even shined up her hoofs. We thought she was just about as pretty as a pony could be, until we got to the show grounds, and saw all the other ponies.

All around were ponies that looked like Star Gazer, and Raven's Wing, high-priced ponies with shiny, really shiny coats, tied next to big shiny trailers. Brooke's face kind of fell, as she looked around. I knew it all must have seemed over-whelming for her, and that she was probably having second thoughts about participating in the show, with all those "fancy" ponies, and "good" riders. "Don't worry about winning," I told her.

"Remember what Miss Joan said, that this will be good experience for the future—besides you'll be in the walk-trot novice class, and the other children in it will have about the same riding ability as you. And don't worry about Sassy not measuring up to the other ponies—pretty is as pretty does—and you know what Sassy can do."

Though timid, and a little shakey, Brooke was ready to try. Sassy, however, the veteran show pony was, as they say, champing at the bit, anxious to perform. Sassy walked into the show ring with her head high. I was hoping that the pony's attitude and self-confidence would be contagious, and be picked up by Brooke. And she was trying very hard to do everything she'd been taught. She was sitting up straight, her heels were down, hands in good position, just over the pommel of the saddle, and her eyes were looking directly ahead.

Booke's parents, and her brother and sister had arrived, and stood beside me on the far side of the ring. They had watched the class ahead of Brooke's, and the kids were all excited about Brooke winning a ribbon.

"I want Brookie to win a pink ribbon," her sister, Laura, said, "then it'll match the ribbons in Sassy's hair."

"Don't be dumb," her brother, Barton, said, "the blue ribbon is first place—so that's what she should win."

"This is her first show," their dad said, "so she probably won't win any ribbon." I smiled and nodded, and picked up Laura so she could see better. "Won't be long before you guys are showing, and then you can win your own ribbons."

At the farm, Brooke had started leading her brother and sister around on Sassy. The younger children loved riding the gentle pony, so dependable was Sassy that she seemed, to them, like a giant windup toy. And Brooke enjoyed being a teacher. I think it helped her to better understand what she needed to do, when riding herself.

"She looks so grownup," her mother said wistfully, as she watched Brooke in the show ring. Her daughter was wearing the new riding jacket she'd bought for her. Around the waist was tied a little square piece of cloth, with the big black number 12 on it. Each rider wore a different number, given to them when they signed up to participate in the show. When the judges selected the winners, they only referred to the riders by the numbers displayed on their backs. Brooke was also wearing the traditional English-style black velvet riding helmet. It made her look taller, and older. "She just doesn't look like a little girl any more," her mother continued.

"I'm sure that right now she still feels like a little girl," I said, "and quite insecure. There's so much to remember. And when you've never done this before, it can be very scary."

There were twelve ponies and riders in this class, and they had all been walking very slowly around the ring. The judge in the middle had just called out, "Reverse, please." And now the riders were all pulling on their reins, to turn their ponies around, to walk the other way. It would be when the judge asked them to trot that the difference in experience would really show.

In a novice, or beginner class, rarely do you have all the riders posting smoothly, on the correct diagonal, while keeping their pony moving at a steady pace.

To post correctly, when riding around a circle, a rider should rise slightly out of the saddle, when the outside front foot of the horse lifts off the ground, and sit down when that same foot goes back down. It is not only proper, but doing that puts the rider in perfect balance with the horse. Just as the rider feels more comfortable, so does the horse.

The reason it's called a diagonal is because, in a trot, at the same time that front foot is lifted up, so is the back foot, on the opposite side. You could draw a diagonal line from the two feet in the air, and the two still on the ground. There is a right and a left diagonal. If you go counter-clockwise in the ring you would post when the *right* front foot goes up. In the other direction, clockwise, it would be the *left* front foot that you'd be rising and falling with.

As a way to remember this Miss Joan says to, "Rise and fall with the leg on the wall."

It's a great deal to think about for any rider, but for children, who haven't been riding very long it's almost impossible to get it all together, at the same time, every time.

"Trot, please!" The judge called out, and all the kids began making clucking noises, and nudging with their heels, as signals for their ponies to trot. Sassy began trotting before the others as if responding to the judge's cue, as much as to Brooke's. And quite possibly she was, because Sassy had done this hundreds of times before. They were at the other end of the ring, but I could see right away that Brooke was on the wrong diagonal. I also knew that she'd never realize it. She would be concentrating so hard, on just continuing to post, that she'd never check the diagonal.

It was when they were on the outside, close to the rail, behind two other ponies, hidden from the view of the judge, that Sassy stumbled ever so slightly. When she collected herself, and started her nice smooth trot again, now right in front of the judge, Brooke was on the correct diagonal. Sassy had forced Brooke into it when she stumbled. "That pony is unbelievable," I whispered to myself.

After that Sassy trotted on without hesitation, and Brooke posted with continuous rhythm and ease, continuing on the *correct* diagonal.

Moving perfectly together, as if they were one, Sassy and Brooke flew past ponies that had slowed to a walk; whose riders were trying to get them trotting again; past riders who had lost their balance, and simply bounced; even past one pair that had come to a complete stop and was parked in the middle of the path. But there were several other riders who were doing very well; riders displaying the experience of having shown before. But because of Sassy's steady pace, Brooke was keeping up with them, and looking equally as good. It was also apparent that she was feeling a great deal more confident than when she had begun.

I suspected that Brooke was feeling so good, about how things were going, that she had even allowed herself to think she might win a ribbon. After all there were six prizes to be awarded.

And so when all the ponies and riders lined up in the center of the ring, and the winners were announced over the loud speaker, you could see Brooke's disappointment, when the announcer, starting at sixth place, got all the way through second place without calling her number. I have to admit that I was feeling disapointment, as well. But I figured that the judge probably knew it was Brooke's first show, and that the judge might think a rider should have more experience before winning something.

Miss Joan had warned, "Don't expect to win a ribbon." Maybe there was even some unwritten rule that prevented first timers from winning. Brooke gave Sassy a pat for the good job the pony had done, and I was pleased to see that Brooke's expression quickly changed to acceptance; a "perhaps next time" kind of look. And she had obviously enjoyed herself by participating in the show, and that was the most important thing. She would want to do it again, because it was fun, not because she had won a ribbon.

"And first place—the blue ribbon," the voice boomed out, "goes to number 12."

Brooke squealed out her surprise and excitement, collapsing onto Sassy's neck and hugging her tight. She had never imagined she might win first place, in her very first show, even though she felt Sassy did deserve it.

Brooke ended up giving that particular blue ribbon to me, because she knew how much it meant to me, that I had bought a pony which could do that for my granddaughter. The ribbon still hangs in my kitchen today.

Eventually there were many other blue ribbons, that Brooke has kept; ribbons she felt she did help to win. But that first one, Brooke always says, "Sassy won all by herself."

The real Sassy's 30th birthday party

Top: Sassy in her birthday hat. Middle: Sassy's cake. Bottom: Sassy and friends.

THREE

❦

On the first day of spring, two years after we bought Sassy, we had a party, a celebration of her thirtieth birthday. We didn't know the actual date of Sassy's birth, but we knew she was to turn 30 years old sometime that year. So we picked March 21st, the first day Brooke ever rode her.

We had party favors, and presents, and a bale of hay decorated like a cake. We used tube icing to spell out HAPPY BIRTHDAY SASSY and stuck carrots in the top to look like candles; not thirty carrots, we didn't want Sassy to get sick at her own party, but enough to look, and taste, good. Sassy didn't blow out the candles on *her* cake, she ate them.

Brooke's family was there, and some of her friends. Charlie Horse was invited to share the cake, as was the pony of Brooke's nearby riding friend, Jessica. Miss Joan came, and we all played games, such as bobbing for apples, and stick-the-tail on Sassy.

We all had a really good time, and I think Sassy did as well. She didn't seem to mind getting older, and she still wasn't showing her age. Brooke was riding more than ever, and always on Sassy. She was still taking lessons, and showing some, although Brooke had decided that she wasn't as interested in showing, as she was in just riding the trails, with me and Charlie Horse, or more often with Jessica and her pony Sonny Boy.

If the girls weren't in school they were with their ponies; at the barn, riding through the woods, or over at Jessica's place. There was a riding ring at Jessica's house, in which the girls had set up a course of jumps. And yes, Sassy was also a good jumper, which made Brooke enjoy it as well. I guess you could say anything that involved Sassy, Brooke found to be fun.

Several weeks after Sassy's party, Brooke was spending the weekend at my house, and Jessica called and asked if Brooke could come over to her house, so they could do some jumping in the ring. Jessica didn't live very far from my farm, about a five-minute drive, or a fifteen-minute ride through the woods. Normally I didn't let Brooke go riding by herself, except around the farm, where I could keep my eye on her. Usually when she went over to Jessica's, I'd go to the trouble to put Sassy on the trailer, and take them over that way, and then, when Brooke was ready to come home, I'd take the trailer back to get them.

But on this day the trailer had a flat tire, and Brooke pleaded with me to let her ride over. It was a beautiful day, and the ground wasn't wet, so Sassy would have firm footing, and there wouldn't be any danger of slipping and falling. Also, Brooke said that'd she'd call the minute she got there, so I wouldn't worry.

She gave me that sad, kind-of-begging, look of hers, and said in a pathetic voice, "You know Sassy will take care of me—you know *she* wouldn't let anything happen to me."

Brooke was nine, almost ten, I reasoned with myself. She was now a good rider, and she was very responsible. So finally I agreed that *if* she promised to be careful, and didn't race through the woods, and *if* she called as soon as she got there, and then called right before she left to come home, so I'd know exactly when she should arrive back at the farm, then she could do it.

When Brooke called, after arriving at Jessica's house, she was laughing hysterically. Apparently she had galloped into Jessica's yard, dismounted in a frenzy, jumping down like a cowboy about to rope a calf, yelling for Jessica to hurry up and hold Sassy, "Come on! Come on" she giggled, "hurry up I gotta call my grandmother—she's timing me —and if I don't call within a certain time she'll have the forest ranger—or Smokey the Bear—or somebody out searching for me." Brooke was trying to tell me over the phone that Jessica had started laughing too, and that made her laugh even more. I could hardly understand a word she was saying. Just listening to her made me laugh, as well. "Okay," I managed to get out, "when you get control of yourself have a good time—and call me when you're ready to leave—and don't wait until it's starting to get dark to come home."

It was about four o'clock when Brooke and Sassy headed for home. She had called me, and said that she was on her way. She felt great, after a wonderful afternoon. Sassy had jumped well, but so had she. She was feeling very confident. "I think I'm ready to try one of the jumping classes in the next show," she had said.

Out on the trail Brooke galloped around the cornfield and slowed to a trot, as she entered the woods on the wide, well used path. The trail was like a fire road, that went up through the trees to the ridge of the hill, and then zigzagged down to a sharp turn at the bottom, which led to a shallow stream crossing. On the other side of the stream the road was pretty straight up through the pines, with an easy ride out onto the power line, which led to the farm.

Brooke and Sassy were in a nice smooth, comfortable trot as they crested the ridge and started down the zigzag trail to the stream. Ordinarily Brooke would have walked down that trail, but she was feeling very self-confident and relaxed, and she was in a hurry to get home. Trotting was so easy, now, she didn't even have to think about what she was doing.

Sassy was picking up speed as they wound down the hill. When they went into the sharp turn at the bottom, right before the stream, they were going pretty fast. Brooke pulled on the right rein a little too soon, and Sassy cut hard, taking the turn more tightly than she should have.

A tree branch loomed ahead. Brooke lunged forward, ducking down as close to Sassy's neck as she could get. The branch swept past Sassy's head and back over Brooke, catching under the front of her riding helmet and lifting it off.

Pulling Sassy to a stop at the edge of the stream, she sat looking down at her helmet, which had rolled down the bank, into the water. It was over by the little rapids.

"Look at that Sassy—my brand-new hat—Mums is going to kill me. She told me I shouldn't wear my show helmet out on the trail. Well I gotta get it."

Brooke rode Sassy out into the stream, to the middle of the shallow crossing. It was only a couple of inches deep; just over Sassy's hoofs. The stream bed had been built up at that point, to allow the jeep-like forestry vehicles to cross.

Well, thought Brooke, *I guess I gotta get my boots wet*. She dismounted, stepping into the water. She took the reins over Sassy's head, and held them in one hand. Brooke felt sure that she didn't really have to hold onto Sassy, that she'd stand by herself, and wait until she got back on again. But just in case something scared her, Brooke thought she'd better hold on. She wouldn't want Sassy running home without her. She knew that would really upset me.

Stepping carefully, Brooke moved toward the helmet. It was wedged between two rocks, just on the other side of the stone ledge, that created the rapids. With the reins stretched out between Sassy and her, Brooke leaned down to try and reach the hat, unaware of what was going on with her pony. Sassy heard something. Her ears pricked up, as she strained to make out the faint, but distinct sound; a high guttural whine from off in the distance, moving rapidly in their direction. Sassy sensed danger. The pony fidgeted, and nickered anxiously.

"Hold on, Sass," Brooke said, without looking back, "hold on girl. I've almost got it." She stooped down, the stream now getting the seat of her pants wet. The sound Sassy heard was getting louder, but all Brooke heard was the rushing water.

"I'm almost there—steady girl." She stretched out as far as she could. Her hand was on the hat, but it was too late. Sassy lurched back, yanking the reins out of Brooke's hands, and charged back across the stream to where they had entered. Brooke stood up in alarm, she now heard it too.

"Get out of the way, Sassy," she screamed, as she splashed through the water toward her pony. Sassy looked back, but didn't move, standing her ground between Brooke and the roaring sound that grew louder. "Move Sassy," she screamed, stumbling and slipping on the wet rocks, and falling down in the water.

The four-wheeler skidded around the blind curve, hit a dirt berm, and was airborn at fifty miles-an-hour, with no way of slowing down, heading straight toward the pony and Brooke. Sassy reared up to meet the screaming monster and its teen-aged driver. Helpless horror flashed across the boy's face as he threw himself off, setting the machine free to slam into the pony in its way.

In a split second there was silence. The four-wheeler lay crumpled and still on the side of the trail. Sassy lay gashed and bleeding at the edge of the stream, the water turning red from her blood. Brooke scrambled to her side.

What life was left would soon be gone. The metal bracket, that had held the rear view mirror on the four-wheeler, had punctured a hole in Sassy's neck. It had probably pierced the windpipe, because she was having trouble breathing. There would never be time to get a vet to save her, not out there in the woods, not now. Brooke knew she had to be brave enough to just try to comfort her pony, and not run for help as she wanted to. Besides, she couldn't leave Sassy alone, not now. She stroked Sassy's neck and rubbed her head. Sassy had been so brave, in protecting her; she would try to be the same. Once again Sassy showed her the way. Though in pain, the pony lay quiet. Brooke, not able to control the tears, cried without sound. The final lesson, Sassy taught this young girl, was the hardest of all. That hidden in the joy of love, is the depth of pain.

From the stream bank the boy stood looking down at the girl and her dying horse. He felt so helpless. Tears also fell from his eyes, forming dusty furrows down his dirty face. He shouldn't have been going as fast as he was, and he knew he never should have gone into that blind curve without slowing down, even stopping, to see what might be up ahead. His father had told him that a dozen times before.

When I rode out on Charlie Horse to see why Brooke wasn't home, when she was supposed to be, and came upon this scene, I knew that I could never make it right. I knew that the most I could do was try to help a young girl heal a broken heart, and a boy deal with a lot of guilt. As for me, there was both; the sadness over losing Sassy, and the guilt for letting Brooke ride out there alone.

EPILOGUE

❦

We buried Sassy near the clump of walnut trees, at the end of the pasture. Mr. Gil brought her out of the woods with his "John Deere" front-end loader. We planted wildflowers on her grave, and a Sassafras tree to mark the spot.

That was ten years ago, and the Sassafras tree is now bushy and quite big. There are days, like today, that I still find myself thinking about Sassy and reflecting on the wonderful qualities of that pony, and the lessons she taught me and Brooke. The lessons about love and kindness, and that a relationship doesn't have to be long-lasting to be important, and to have a powerful affect on your life. Also, whenever I've started to feel old, wondering about my usefulness, in this youth-oriented world, I think about Sassy and how she used her age and experience to teach, and bring joy to a little girl.

As I sit in my favorite chair, looking out of the window at the empty barn, I hear the back door open and close. "Mums, are you home?"

It's Brooke. She's going off to college. This is an exciting day, but sort of sad, as well, because I'll miss her not being around. The years have gone by so quickly. But she has grown into such a wonderful young woman, there can be no regrets.

"Come in dear—come in and sit down."

Brooke has a bunch of wildflowers in her hand. "I thought you might like these—not too many left—this late in the summer. They're from me and Sassy." Brooke paused a moment before continuing. "I told Sassy that I'm going to college— that I'm going to be a vet—that maybe someday I'll have a chance to save the life of a pony, as wonderful as she was—and maybe that will be a payback for all she did for me—for saving my life." Brooke handed me the flowers, and said, "But, I don't know how I'll ever be able to pay you back—I love you so much."

Tears of emotion clouded my eyes, and my throat tightened, making it impossible to speak.

Imagine me, Elizabeth "Mums" Wordley not able to talk. But my heart sang out—remembering—a child and a pony, and unconditional love, and for that there is no payment due.

Jack and Susan with their dog, Angel.
Photo by: Granddaughter Emily

ABOUT THE AUTHOR

A former television reporter/anchor, Susan White-Bowden now spends her time writing, lecturing and occasionally teaching. Among her favorite audiences are school children, especially the fifth-grade *Just Say No* clubs.

Susan's daily activities include caring for the animals on the family farm, and spending a part of each day with her grandchildren. The animals and children provide endless love and adventure, and, as with this book, things to ponder and write about.

Susan is married to Washington D.C. television reporter/anchor Jack Bowden, and, even though Jack has contributed to all of Susan's books, they hope someday to devote more time to writing together.